To Anna and Charlotte, with love

T.C xx

WILLOW VALLEY

Chapter 1

It was a bright, sunny day in Willow Valley. Spring had come at last! Daisies were popping up everywhere, baby lambs were bouncing in the fields, and the hills were covered in a carpet of soft green grass.

All through the winter the meadows and woods had been quiet, dark and cold. But now they were filled with happy children skipping about in the bluebells. Cave-house doors were open wide as the grown-ups swept the thick winter cobwebs away.

Riley, a little toffee-coloured mouse, was down at Buttonoak Mill. He was fishing for tadpoles in the big millpond. With him were his two best friends – Starla, a smiley, fluffy-faced badger and a roly-poly hedgehog called Horatio Spark.

Holding their jam jars by their thin wire handles, the three friends dipped them into the water. When they lifted the jars back out they were full of busy little tadpoles. They looked like wriggly blackcurrants with tails!

Riley was going to take the tadpoles
to live in his garden pond. He'd spent
all of yesterday cleaning it especially.
The friends planned to meet there every
day and watch the tadpoles turn into
frogs. They couldn't *wait* to see them
grow legs and hop about!

"Let's go!" said Riley, and the three headed off, carefully holding their jam jars. As they walked along beside the river, the water twinkled in the bright spring sunshine.

"And *look*," smiled Starla, "the first butterfly of the year!"

The river led on to the village square. The friends passed the tall fir tree standing in the middle. Behind it were some little shops. There was a toy shop which was owned by Riley's grandpa, a baker's full of delicious cakes, and also Library Cave where they went after school to read stories.

The shops had their doors open wide. Riley's grandpa's shop smelled of wood and polish.

"Beeswax polish!" Riley said. All of Percy Lightfoot's toys were made from wood, which Riley helped him polish until they shone.

The baker's next door smelled of warm currant buns. Riley's little pink nose sniffed the air. "Mmmm," he said, "those buns smell really yummy!"

As the friends looked at the cakes in the window, they heard a big, rumbling sound.

"What was that?" gasped Starla. "It sounded like thunder."

"No, that's just my *tummy*, silly!" grinned Horatio. "It always rumbles when it's time for a little something."

The friends hadn't brought any money for cakes, so they walked on up the hill. Riley's cave-house was right at the very top.

"Do you think," said Horatio (whose tummy was still rumbling), "your mum might have *baked* a little something? Ginger cake, perhaps?" That was his favourite.

"Maybe," shrugged Riley. "I know that she was going to bake something for the Daisy Chain Party on Saturday."

"Oh, the Daisy Chain Party!" squealed Starla. "I can't wait for that!"

"And the Great Egg Hunt!" Horatio cried excitedly. Today was Thursday, so the fun was just *two* days away!

Saturday was going to be a very special day for everyone in Willow Valley. It would be a day full of celebration to welcome the arrival of spring.

Tomorrow night, when everyone was fast asleep, the Hoppity Bunny would hide painted eggs all over the valley.

Then on Saturday morning the Great Egg Hunt would take place. All the children would wear special springtime headbands and search for the pretty hidden eggs!

Riley really loved the egg hunt. The Hoppity Bunny hid the eggs in all sorts of funny places. Horatio enjoyed it too. But he preferred the *chocolate* eggs that the children made to give as gifts on the morning of the egg hunt.

"Hey, guys," he said, "*guess what –* my dad said he'd help us make our chocolate eggs tomorrow."

"Yippee!" cried Riley and Starla. That sounded great.

They were also having a sleepover at Riley's on Friday night. They planned to stay up to see the Hoppity Bunny because no one really knew what he looked like. Horatio had tried to spot him every year but had always fallen asleep after his cocoa. This time, the others would be there to help him stay awake!

On the evening of the egg hunt, the Daisy Chain Party would be the perfect end to the day. It would happen on one of the Willow Valley narrowboats. This year it was going to be on the *Dragonfly*, a bottle-green boat painted with lacy-winged dragonflies.

The party always started after afternoon tea and went on really late. There would be music, and games, and cake! There would even be a *tree* on the boat – a blossom tree in a great big flowerpot. The children would decorate it with the painted eggs they'd found at the egg hunt.

"I hope there's ginger cake at the party," said Horatio.

"There *will* be," smiled Starla. "There'll be everything!"

She loved all the bunting that would hang on the boat. She and her mum had been busily sewing it all week. There would be garlands of daisy chains too, and jugs of spring flowers on the long party table, and pretty coloured lanterns everywhere!

"Come on," said Riley, as they reached his garden gate. "Let's get these tadpoles into the pond, and then we can start making our headbands for the Great Egg Hunt!"

Chapter 2

The friends popped the tadpoles into Riley's pond. Then they sat amongst the buttercups and planned the spring headbands they would make. . .

"I'm putting flowers on mine," said Starla. "I'm going to make them from buttons. I think I'll do daffodils because I really like yellow."

"I'm going to do a feathery headband," said Riley. "Because birds make nests in the spring."

"Well," said Horatio, puffing out his chest, "my headband's having a *frog* on it!" The tadpoles had given him this idea.

"It's going to be a big frog, too!" he smiled. "So I'm going to need lots of green tissue paper."

Riley said they should get his making-things box. There were lots of things in there that they could use.

They hurried in and found the box in the dresser. Then they took it back out to the garden and Riley opened the lid.

Riley's making-things box was like a treasure chest filled with sparkly bits and bobs. There were shiny wrappers,

sequins and wool, and all sorts of
buttons and feathers. There was ribbon,
and beads, and pots of bright glitter too.

As they looked for Horatio's tissue paper, Riley's little sister, Mimi-Rose, skipped out dressed up in her bunny suit. She was carrying a basket filled with scrunched-up balls of paper.

"I'm the *Hoppity Bunny*!" squeaked Mimi-Rose. "And I'm hiding all my eggs! No peeping or that's cheating!" she giggled.

She bounced around them. "Boing! Boing! Boing!" Then she stopped and knelt on the grass.

"What are you making?" Mimi-Rose asked.

"Great Egg Hunt headbands," said Riley.

"Oh!" smiled his sister. "I want to do that too!"

They began to gather all the different things they needed for the decorating. Starla found lots of big yellow buttons and some smaller orange ones for the centres of her daffodils. Riley picked out lots of soft and colourful feathers. Mimi-Rose chose some shiny red wrappers and started to glue on black spots.

"Look! I'm making ladybirds!" she said.

"Isn't this fun?" Horatio grinned, as he scrunched up his tissue paper into two huge balls – one for his frog's head and one for its body.

When no one was looking, he stuck a small white feather on the end of Riley's tail.

"Hey, Riley," cried Horatio, "*guess what* – you're turning into a chicken!"

"What do you mean?" Riley asked.

"Your tail!" snorted Starla. "You've sprouted a feather, look!"

Riley looked. "Oh no!" he gasped. But suddenly he worked out who had done it and his gasp turned into a grin.

"Buck! Buck!" Riley clucked as he strutted like a chicken.

"Funny Riley!" giggled Mimi-Rose.

They were happily working on their headbands when Riley's mum came out with a picnic basket. It was the very first picnic of the year.

"Yippee!" cheered Riley. He *loved* picnics!

Everyone piled on to the big checked rug Riley's mum had laid out and waited patiently as she emptied the picnic basket.

"Mmm!" they said. The food looked ever so yummy!

There were pasties, warm bread rolls and cheese. There was sparkling elderflower cordial too, made from last summer's elderberry flowers.

Everyone helped themselves to the
goodies. They especially liked the
biscuits Riley's mum had baked. They
were shaped like butterflies and
all around their iced wings were
little daisy sweets.

"I made them for the Daisy Chain
Party," she said. "But I saved a few for
you. So how are you getting on with
your headbands?"

"We haven't *quite* finished them yet,"
replied Riley. "But they're starting to
look really good."

As they ate, the friends decided to
finish off their headbands in Bluebell

Wood. All the bluebells would be out now and it would be so pretty!

After lunch they gathered up their things and headed off down the hill. Riley didn't need to be home until teatime, so that gave him lots of time to finish his headband.

When they arrived at Bluebell Wood, the friends got quite a surprise. All of their *other* friends were there making headbands too!

"Hi!" called Abigail Bright, a red squirrel. "Starla – come and see my headband!"

Starla hurried over. "Wow," she said, "that's great!"

Abigail was filling her headband with butterflies made out of real flower petals. Abigail's best friend, Posy Vole, showed Starla her headband too. Posy was making little lambs from white cherry blossom.

"What's on yours?" Posy asked Starla. So Starla held out her headband.

"It's not finished yet," she said, "but these buttons are meant to be daffodils. Riley's using feathers and Horatio's making a big fat frog!"

The boys came over with Bramble Bunny and little Digby Mole. Bramble hadn't started his headband yet because

he'd been too busy playing. But Digby
had done little bead beetles and wiggly
pink worms made from wool. Digby
was very good at making things.

Horatio popped his headband on. His big messy frog wobbled, then flopped down over his eyes. "Ooops!" he grinned. "I think it needs a bit more glue."

A large group of animals were sitting in the bluebells, all working away on their headbands. Riley and his friends went over to join them and stayed there chatting, glittering and gluing until the headbands were finally finished.

"Let's play stuck-in-the-mud!" suggested Riley when everything was tidied away.

"Or stuck-in-the-*bluebells* today,"

laughed Horatio. He begged the others to let him be "It". "Look – I can be a monster frog!" he cried, putting on his headband. "And you are all the *flies* for my supper! Ribbit! Ribbit! Roar!"

Everyone raced off through the bluebells screaming, "The monster frog's coming! Arrgh!"

"Don't let him get you!" shouted Bramble Bunny. "Run!"

If the monster frog tugged their tail, then they were stuck-in-the-bluebells. They'd have to stand still until someone "unstuck" them by swooping under their outstretched paws.

"You'll *never* catch me, monster frog!" giggled Abigail, as Horatio *just* missed her tail.

"He's coming!" gulped Digby.

"Eeek!" squeaked Phoebe Badger.

"Watch out, guys!" Posy chuckled.

Shrieks of excitement and big booming croaks filled the warm spring air as the prickly monster frog caught fly after fly. . .

"Got you, Digby!"

"Got you, Posy!"

"Got you, Riley!" croaked Horatio. Soon every last fly was stuck-in-the-bluebells.

"Now let's play hide-and-seek!" cried

Horatio. "Come on!"

After hide-and-seek they played leapfrog too. Then they all piled on to the old stone bridge and played poohsticks in the stream. It felt so good to be out in the sunshine again!

By teatime they were quite worn

out and wandered home carrying their headbands. Horatio's looked very crumpled now, as he'd been wearing it all afternoon. He didn't seem to mind, though.

"Monster frogs are meant to look like that!" he grinned.

Riley had had so much fun. And tomorrow there'd be even *more*. First, making yummy chocolate eggs, then having a sleepover at his house. And they might even get to spot the Hoppity Bunny!

Chapter 3

On Friday morning Riley woke bright and early. It was another sunny day! He hurried downstairs and wolfed down his porridge.

"Slow down," laughed his mum. But Riley couldn't wait to get to Horatio's house. He drank up his milk, licked his whiskers clean and then pattered over to the door.

"See you later!" he called, waving goodbye. He was staying at Horatio's for lunch.

"Bye," smiled his mum. "Have a lovely day."

"I will!"

Riley hurried outside and ran down the hill, his whiskers blowing out behind him. "Boing!" he giggled as he bunny-hopped over the daisies.

At the bottom of the hill, three big narrowboats bobbed about on the water. The animals of Willow Valley used these boats for their market trips, when they sailed downriver to sell their home-made goods.

Soon they'd be going on the first trip of the year to sell lemon cakes and primrose perfume. They'd also sell bundles of dried sticks for those who loved crackling fires on chilly spring nights.

The *Whirligig* was at the front. This was a dark blue boat with little beetles and pale pink roses painted around its windows. Now it had flowerpots up on deck too, filled with sunny daffodils.

Behind it was the *Kingfisher*. This was a smart, sky blue boat with a kingfisher painted on its bow. Its feathers were all shades of blues and greens, and in its pointy beak it held a fish.

The *Kingfisher* was Riley's favourite boat. But today he couldn't take his eyes off the *Dragonfly* as everyone got it ready for the Daisy Chain Party tomorrow night.

Hector Rabbit, who was much older than Riley, was scrubbing down the deck. Hector's friend Benjamin Bobtail was there too, helping Mumford Mole carry a huge flowerpot up the gangplank. In this pot was the blossom tree they would hang their painted eggs on at the party!

Riley spotted Starla's grandpa, Willoughby White-Whiskers, hanging

up a banner with Podrick Hare. It said
The Daisy Chain Party in swirly
green writing.

"Mr White-Whiskers!" called Riley.
"Is Starla there, please? We're going to
Horatio's to make our chocolate eggs
today!"

"Ah yes," Mr White-Whiskers smiled
back down. "I remember!"

He and Podrick finished hanging the
banner. Then Willoughby popped down
below deck and a few moments later, he
came back with Starla.

"Hi, Riley!" she called, hurrying down
the gangplank.

They skipped away under the willow trees. The sun was warm, and chirpy little birds were building their nests in the treetops.

Riley and Starla followed the path of the river. Then they climbed a steep hill to Horatio's house at the top.

Horatio's garden was filled with little hedgehogs all tumbling about in the grass. Horatio had more little brothers and sisters than you could count!

The little hedgehogs dragged Riley and Starla into the house, and down a long tunnel to the underground kitchen.

"You're here!" cried Horatio.

"Chocolate egg time, then!" grinned

his dad.

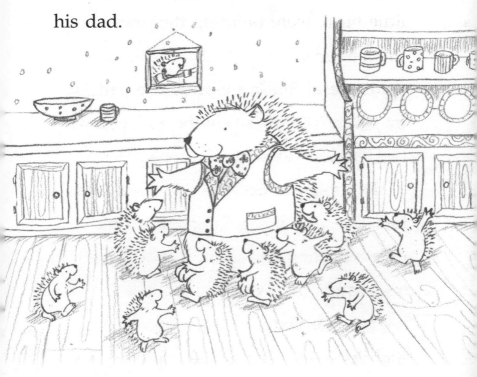

Mr Spark was as round as a cricket

ball, with rosy cheeks and a twinkling

smile. He wore bright bow ties all year round. His winter one had big white snowflakes on it, his summer one had bumblebees, his autumn bow tie was filled with bright leaves. But his spring one, which he was wearing today, was green with yellow dots and daisies.

Mr Spark opened the dresser drawer and took out a huge stack of aprons. "Here we are!" he grinned as he handed them out.

The friends all put their aprons on, then helped the little ones into theirs. It was tricky getting *anything* over a headful of prickles!

"Now all wash your paws," Mr Spark told them. "Nice and clean, mind!"

"OK!" said lots of little voices. "We will!"

When everyone's paws had been washed and dried, it was time to start the cooking. Mr Spark called them over to the kitchen table. He stood the little ones on long wooden benches so that they'd be able to see.

"First we must break up the chocolate," he said. He handed them each a big bar of chocolate. The little ones started to nibble it at once, and even Horatio took a few sneaky bites.

"Nooo!" laughed Mr Spark. "You
break it with your *paws*, not your teeth!"

When the chocolate was finally in nice
small bits, they popped it into a bowl.

"The stove is very hot," said Mr
Spark, "so *I'll* do the melting."

He sat the bowl on top of a pan of hot water and stirred the chocolate as it melted. As he did, little noses sniffed the air. It smelled yummy!

When the chocolate looked like a shiny brown sea, Mr Spark placed the bowl back on to the table. Now the melted chocolate could be spooned into the egg moulds.

"But, Mr Spark," Riley said, "these egg moulds only look like *half* an egg to me."

Horatio's dad explained that when the chocolate had cooled and become hard again they would put *two* egg halves together to make a whole egg.

"See, Riley – like this!" he said.

"Oh, I remember," Starla smiled. "Me and my mum did that last year!"

Mr Spark helped the bigger children to spoon in the melted chocolate. The little ones had to watch, as the chocolate was still quite hot.

As they were waiting for the chocolate to go hard, Horatio's mum came in. She'd been to the baker's to get some bread for lunch. She'd also bought some currant buns.

"I *love* currant buns!" Riley nodded, licking his lips excitedly.

"Let's eat them in the garden," said Horatio, and they hurried out.

Everyone sat under the beech tree and gobbled up their currant buns. Mrs Spark also brought out a big basket of bread and lots and lots of cheese. Riley liked having lunch at Horatio's so much!

When they had finished, it was time to check their eggs. The chocolate had gone nice and hard, so now they could decorate them!

Mr Spark took the eggs from the moulds and stuck the two halves together with some more melted chocolate.

"And here are some icing bags," he said. He also gave them sprinkles and sweets. "Now you can decorate the eggs any way you like!"

Using the icing bags was such great fun. It was just like squeezing out toothpaste!

"Whoops!" grinned Horatio, as he squeezed too hard and the icing shot out and hit his nose. "Mmmm," he said as he licked it off, *delicious!*

The little ones liked sucking icing straight from the nozzle and very little went on their eggs. But Riley and Starla tried to make their eggs look good, as they were going to be presents.

Riley iced zigzags all over his eggs in as many colours as he could. He also did flowers with jelly sweets in the middle, which looked yummy!

Starla decided to do pictures on hers. One of them was of the Hoppity Bunny holding a basket of eggs. Another was dotted with fluffy yellow chicks and had a big orange ribbon wrapped around its middle.

When the eggs were all iced, the friends did the washing up. Horatio filled the sink with bright rainbow bubbles which floated into the air. Then the little ones jumped about, popping them on their sharp prickles!

It took a while before the kitchen looked back to normal, but in the end it did. Mrs Spark had some baskets for them to put their eggs in. Each was beautifully lined with soft green leaves, and ribbons of ivy were wound around the handles. The friends would take the eggs to Riley's house to give out tomorrow morning after their sleepover.

Horatio just had to pack his rucksack and then they'd be ready to go. He popped in his toothbrush, his pyjamas and a ginger cake. "For a little midnight snack," he explained. Then they picked up their baskets of eggs and off they went.

As they walked to Riley's, Starla showed the boys a book she had about the Hoppity Bunny. It had lots of tips on how to spot him.

"But I wonder what he *looks* like?" Riley said, as they skipped off down the hill. Fingers crossed they'd find out later on!

Chapter 4

That night, after supper at Riley's house, the friends put up a tent in his bedroom.

They had wanted to camp out in the garden but it was still a bit too chilly in the evenings. Riley's mum had said they could camp *inside* instead. They could still look out for the Hoppity Bunny from Riley's bedroom window.

While they waited for the bunny, they drew pictures of what it might look like. Starla's Hoppity Bunny had fluffy white ears, big paws for hopping and a daffodil in its hair.

Starla drew it hopping around her garden. "My bunny's fast too," she nodded. "It can hop around the whole wide world in ten seconds!"

Riley's Hoppity Bunny was brown and white with lots of curly whiskers. "And it can hop *right up to the moon*!" he boasted.

Finally, they looked at Horatio's bunny. It looked like a wobbly jelly.

"That's why he's such a good hopper," said Horatio. "The wobblier you are, the higher you can bounce, everyone knows that!"

As the friends carried on with their drawings, Horatio kept sneaking bites of his ginger cake when nobody was looking. Camping always made him *very* hungry!

Then Starla took out her bunny book and everyone started to read it. The book had puzzles, mazes, and word searches too. It was great!

First, they did a couple of the springtime word searches. Then, after figuring out a really hard maze, they read a few facts about the Hoppity Bunny.

"It says the bunny likes *cake*," grinned

Horatio. "And that carrot cake
is its favourite!"

"Maybe we should leave out some
cake, then?" said Riley.

"Good idea!" Starla nodded.

The problem was, the only cake they
had was Horatio's ginger cake. And
oddly, that looked much smaller than it
had when he'd packed it earlier!

"Oh well," shrugged Riley, picking it
up, "I'm sure it'll be OK." But as he
went to pop it outside the tent door. . .

"*Guys –*" whispered Riley "– did you
hear that? I think there's something
outside!"

"What – outside our *tent*?" Horatio whispered, his prickles all of a quiver.

"No, out in the *garden*," Riley whispered back. "That sounded like a twig snap to me!"

"It must be the Hoppity Bunny!" gasped Starla. *"Let's look!"*

The friends tiptoed over to the bedroom window. The moon was big and silvery bright as three pairs of eyes peeped outside. A dusting of dewdrops sparkled on the grass like diamonds.

"There!" squealed Starla, pointing a paw. "Look – it's the Hoppity Bunny!"

They looked down the garden to the dry stone wall. There, sticking up behind it, were two fluffy brown *rabbit* ears.

"The Hoppity Bunny's ears!" Horatio cried.

As the Hoppity Bunny walked on, his
ears bobbed along behind the wall. But
Starla looked puzzled. Something just
wasn't right.

"Hang on," she said, "why is he
walking? Surely the *Hoppity* Bunny's
meant to . . . *hop*?"

"Hmmm," muttered Riley. Starla was
right.

Then the Hoppity Bunny walked past
the open gate and the friends saw the
rest of him too.

"Oh look," groaned Riley. "It's just
Hector Rabbit!"

"Silly us!" Horatio giggled. "Fancy

thinking Hector was the Hoppity Bunny!"

Riley opened the window.

"Hi, Hector!" they called.

Hector stopped, looked up, and waved.

"Why are you out so late?" asked Starla.

"I've been helping get the *Dragonfly* ready," called Hector. "For the party tomorrow night. We've only just finished. It's taken all day! Now we're all heading home, see?"

Hector pointed behind him. Walking up the hill were lots of grown-ups with lanterns.

"We're off home for supper and bed now," said Hector. "See you tomorrow at the egg hunt! Night, night!"

The friends said goodnight and Riley closed his window. As he did, his mum came in carrying a tray. On it were three steaming mugs.

"Cocoa!" she called, and the friends licked their lips.

"Oh yum!"

They drank their cocoa inside the tent. It was getting very late now.

"I'm still not tired," Horatio announced.

"Nor me," said Riley, stretching.

"I am, a little bit," Starla nodded. "But I'd *still* like to wait up and see the Hoppity Bunny."

"Mmmm. . ." yawned the boys. "Us too."

They rubbed their eyes. It was warm in the tent. Warm, and dark, and cosy.

They decided to get into their sleeping bags. Just for a minute or two. They weren't going to go to sleep, just have a small rest.

"Ahhhh," breathed Riley. His pillow was so soft and his sleeping bag was snuggly. "I'm really . . . not sleepy . . . at . . . all. . ."

With that, his heavy eyelids closed and deep, happy snores filled the tent. All three friends were now fast asleep, dreaming of sunshine and eggs!

Chapter 5

"Riley! It's morning!" Horatio cried.
"And the Hoppity Bunny's been!"

Riley opened one sleepy eye.

"Starla!" Horatio shouted. "Quick!
Wake up!"

As Starla gave a big yawn, Riley
looked round the tent. In his basket of
chocolate eggs there was now a *painted*
egg too! And beside it was a note from
the Hoppity Bunny.

Wakey wakey, sleepy-head,
now it's time for fun!
Up you get and off you hop,
the Great Egg Hunt's begun!

"Wow!" cried Riley. "Look at this!"

Horatio and Starla each had a note too,

along with a painted egg.

But before the Great Egg Hunt could start there were *chocolate* eggs to give out. Riley took two out of his basket.

"One for you," he said to Starla. "And one for you, Horatio."

"Hurray!" cheered Horatio, taking his egg and sniffing the dreamy chocolate. Then in two big bites the egg was in his tummy. "Thanks, Riley!"

Next Starla gave out her eggs. Horatio's was the one with the Hoppity Bunny on, and Riley got the one with the big orange bow and fluffy chicks.

That just left Horatio's eggs. As he handed them out his cheeks turned bright pink. There were little holes all over the eggs. Rather like they'd been nibbled.

"I was just . . . a tiny bit . . . peckish," said Horatio. "Sorry!"

He hung his head and stared at his feet. He did look very sad.

"Don't worry," said Starla.

"Yeah," grinned Riley. "There's still lots of chocolate left!"

They took the eggs and nibbled them too. What was left was really tasty! As they were allowed a special lie-in on the morning of the Great Egg Hunt, they had woken up late and were *very* hungry.

"And I think I smell *pancakes* as well!" cried Riley. "Follow me!"

Grabbing their baskets, they pattered downstairs, where they found Riley's mum tossing pancakes. They *always* had pancakes on Great Egg Hunt day. Riley loved them!

"Hi, Mum!" he said brightly. "Hi, Mimi-Rose! Did the Hoppity Bunny leave anything in your basket?"

"He did! He did!" his little sister squealed. "Look!"

Mimi-Rose held up her basket, where a painted egg sat amongst all the little chocolate ones. It was lilac with bright yellow butterflies on.

"Oh!" said Starla. "How pretty!"

Riley took a chocolate egg out of his basket. "For you, Mimi-Rose," he said to her.

He passed it over and Mimi-Rose smiled. The shiny brown chocolate was iced with pink dots. There were lots of pretty flowers on it too.

"And I've got an egg for *you*," she said. "And for Starla, and Horatio!" She'd made them with her mum when Riley was at Horatio's yesterday.

Proudly, Mimi-Rose gave out her eggs. They all looked very different. Starla's was made from shiny dark chocolate with wibbly stars iced all over it. Horatio's was milk chocolate dotted with sweets. Last of all, Riley's egg was creamy white chocolate with a heart made from pink chocolate buttons.

"And who wants some pancakes?" Riley's mum called over.

"Me!" cried everyone.

They hurried to the table, which looked very pretty. There was a big jug of daffodils beside the red teapot. The best plates and mugs were out too.

Everyone took a pancake and loaded it with toppings. Starla had blueberries, Riley had honey, Mimi-Rose had strawberry jam, and Horatio had a little bit of everything, of course!

As they ate, Riley's mum gave out *her* chocolate eggs. Riley's had a little train on the front piped in bright blue icing. It was puffing out clouds of marshmallow smoke – all soft and fluffy and white.

"Thanks, Mum!" said Riley, and he gave her an egg too. On it he'd iced a mummy sheep with two baby lambs in the daisies beside her.

"How lovely!" smiled his mum, and she gave him a hug. "Thank you, Riley."

It was nearly time for the Great Egg Hunt. It would be starting in ten minutes at the top of Hoot Hill.

The Hoppity Bunny had been busy in the night, hiding all his painted eggs. They were always in really tricky places to find. Riley liked that, though. It made the hunt all the more exciting!

"Come on then!" he cried. They raced upstairs, got dressed and popped on their springtime headbands. Riley's mum gave them each a little basket to put in all the eggs they found. Then out they went into the bright spring sunshine!

They raced past the tadpoles in the garden pond and out through the gate to the field.

"Wait for me!" cried Riley's mum,

dashing behind. The grown-ups liked to watch the egg hunt too.

Riley led the way down the hill, through a sea of dandelion clocks. Each one was big and fluffy and round – like a moon filled with soft white wishes. When the breeze blew, the wishes puffed off – up, up, into the sky. Then away they floated over the hedgerows like fairies!

When the friends reached the top of Hoot Hill, they saw it was very crowded. Rosy-cheeked hedgehogs were tumbling in the flowers, squirrels were leaping through the trees, and some big-boy badgers had made a see-saw on a tree stump.

Riley spotted Bramble and Digby Mole. Digby was jigging with excitement.

"Oh!" he squeaked. "I really love the egg hunt!"

Then Abigail Bright and Posy Vole skipped up. They had tied coloured ribbons on the handles of their baskets. Abigail had lots in her bushy tail too.

"I like your ribbons," Starla said to them.

"Thanks!" the girls replied, and they gave her some ribbons to tie on her basket too.

Suddenly, a whistle sounded behind them.

"Time for the egg hunt!" Willoughby White-Whiskers called. He gathered the children at the top of the hill.

"Good!" he smiled, his eyes twinkling. "Right – three, two, one . . . GO!"

There was a patter of paws as loud as thunder as children scurried off everywhere.

"To the barn!" cried Riley. "There are *always* eggs round there!"

Squealing, the friends raced off to the barn and started to search through the grass.

"There!" shouted Starla. "By the barn door. I see one!"

They bounded over to the barn door where the Hoppity Bunny had hidden two eggs. An orange one sat in a big clump of primroses. Beside the flowers was an old water barrel and Horatio fished one out of there. Their egg hunt had started off really well!

"Let's try the orchard next," said Starla. They hurried there and started to search. Soon Riley spotted a red egg in the apple tree. It looked just like an apple! The Hoppity Bunny was really very clever.

Riley scurried up the tree, grabbed the egg and threw it down to his friends. Horatio caught it and put it into Riley's basket for him.

"Where next, then?" asked Starla, as Riley climbed back down.

"Buttonoak Mill!" panted Digby Mole, racing by like a whirlwind. "There are *tons* of eggs down there!" he called back.

"Bramble said so!"

The friends dashed off to Buttonoak Mill. On the way they passed the allotments where Podrick Hare was planting sweet peas.

"Any eggs around here, Mr Hare?" asked Riley.

"Who knows?" grinned Podrick. "Have a look if you like."

"*Thanks!*"

They searched around and found lots of eggs. There were three under a stack of upturned flowerpots. There were two in the watering can. And there were *five* in Podrick's potting shed, hidden

amongst his tools. There was *even* an

egg in one of Podrick's old wellies!

The friends thanked Podrick, then

hurried on to the mill, where they found

four eggs in the rushes.

"And look!" said Starla, peeping under an old rowing boat. There were more painted eggs than they could count!

The egg hunt went on, and on, and on – nobody wanted it to stop! Finally, when tummies were starting to rumble, the children wandered down to Buttercup Meadow, where afternoon tea was being served.

"Wow, scones!" cried Horatio. *"With blackberry jam and cream!"*

As everyone tucked in, the children made daisy chains to drape around the *Dragonfly* at the Daisy Chain Party. They wouldn't have to wait much longer, as it was happening right after tea.

And before they knew it, Willoughby called "Come on then! Let's all walk to the boat."

"Yippee!" cheered Riley. It was party time at last!

Chapter 6

The *Dragonfly* had never looked prettier as everyone skipped on for the party.

"Look!" squeaked Riley. There was bunting everywhere, fluttering in the breeze. And the long party table was filled with plates of sandwiches, and cakes, and dainty iced biscuits to eat later.

The children hung their daisy chains all around the boat. They were still wearing their springtime headbands and their baskets were full of pretty painted eggs.

"Ooooh!" said Starla. "There's the special tree!"

She pointed to where the blossom tree stood in its enormous flowerpot. Last year it had been a pink cherry-blossom tree but this year it was a white one.

Suddenly some happy music began and the friends turned round to look. Mumford Mole was up at the back of the boat playing his fiddle. Then Willoughby joined in on his old tin whistle.

Horatio's mum and dad had instruments too. Mrs Spark was strumming a little banjo and Mr Spark had a bright gold horn. Each time he blew it his prickles pinged up so he looked like a rosy-cheeked pincushion. It was so funny!

Hector Rabbit was on drums. As he banged away his ears flew about, like long socks blowing in the wind.

"Come on," Starla said to the boys, "it's time for the songs!"

Everyone gathered round and Mumford started off with a song the friends sometimes sang at school. It was one about the Hoppity Bunny hiding his eggs.

Riley and his friends remembered the tune but they hadn't sung the song for a while. Not since this time last spring, a whole year ago.

Horatio started to sing along. But he didn't know all the words, so he filled in the bits he didn't know with big booming laaaas. . .

*"Where will he hide them? What is inside them? Those **la, la, la, la,** pretty painted eggs! The **la, la, la, la** – hopping – hiding, **la-la-la-la-la-la-la-laaaaa!"***

Soon *all* the animals of Willow Valley were singing loudly – songs about daffodils, songs about eggs, songs about lambs in the fields! And as they sang, the afternoon sun was slowly turning from buttercup yellow to a warm, deep shade of gold.

After the singing, some gentler music was played and the children all paraded around showing off their springtime headbands.

Lots of the headbands were decorated with flowers – paper flowers, material flowers and button flowers, like on Starla's.

Other headbands had little eggs on. Not real ones, of course, but rolled-up balls of tissue paper.

Bramble Bunny had rabbits going all around his headband. He had cut them from a long strip of folded-up paper so that they all looked the same. They were joined at the paws, like they were holding hands!

Starla liked Phoebe Badger's headband, which had chicks on it, made from yellow pom-poms. But the boys thought the woolly worms on Digby's headband was the coolest idea of all!

The parade ended with the children hanging their painted eggs on the branches of the blossom tree. Horatio hung his *headband* on there too, seeing as his frog had fallen off during the songs!

Now it was time for some party games, starting with musical chairs. Riley, who was small and very nippy, was really good at this game. But he knew that Abigail was speedy too. Riley supposed that, being a squirrel, she was used to zipping up trees. He'd have to dive on to those chairs pretty fast to beat *her*.

Mumford Mole appeared with a big bag of instruments as he was doing the music for the game. "Right then, who's ready for some fun?" he asked.

"Me!" everyone cried.

Mr Mole popped his fiddle under his silky black chin and started to play some music. As he did, all the children began marching around the chairs.

Riley's ears were pricked up as he listened hard for the moment that the music stopped. "Oooh!" he squeaked. This was *so* exciting!

The children marched round and round the chairs. Then suddenly it went all quiet.

"Arggggh!" screamed everyone, diving for a chair.

"Quick!"

"Run!"

Digby was the one left without a chair, so he was the first one out.

"Never mind, Digby," said Mr Mole. He gave him a tambourine. "You can come and help with the music instead."

The game carried on until, at last, only Abigail and Riley were left in.

"Go, Riley!" boomed Horatio.

"Go, Abigail!" Posy shouted.

Mumford's band was enormous now. Everyone who was out had been given an instrument from his bag and was helping with the music.

They started to play a loud, clangy song as Riley and Abigail marched around the last chair. When they got to the *front* of the chair they slowed down to be close if the music stopped. When they got to the back of it, though, they raced round like the wind!

And then – at last – it went all quiet. Riley and Abigail both flew for the chair seat. But Abigail's big, bushy tail was in the way and Riley couldn't see a thing!

"I did it!" cried Abigail, diving on to the seat. A cheering Posy skipped over to see her.

"Hard luck, Riley," Starla said, and Horatio patted his back.

"It's OK," said Riley. The game had been fun, and now it was time for the party food!

"Come on, then!" cried Horatio, rubbing his tummy. He was starving!

The lanterns were lit and candles flickered in jars as everyone sat down and helped themselves to food – crunchy spring vegetables fresh from the fields, cakes, and sandwiches, and cherry ice cream with butterfly biscuits made by Riley's mum! As they nibbled, the friends all talked about their wonderful day.

"I've loved *everything*," Riley beamed, his whiskers dripping in ice cream.

"Me too," said Starla, and Horatio licked his spoon and nodded.

Later on, Willoughby took the boat downriver as a very special springtime treat. The riverbank was lined with willow trees, all filled with bright new leaves.

Their branches bent down into the water, stroking the side of the *Dragonfly*. And the darkening fields were filled with little lambs, still bouncing!

The apricot sky had ribbons of purple when the boat stopped at Buttonoak Mill. Riley thought of the tadpoles in his garden pond. Maybe they'd have little legs by the time he got home!

When the first tiny stars winked in the sky, Martha Rabbit brought out a cake she had baked in the shape of

the Hoppity Bunny. It was iced in pale
buttercream, and had lovely tall ears,
two shiny black eyes, and a small pink
marshmallow nose.

"So *that's* what the Hoppity Bunny
looks like!" laughed Horatio.

As they ate their cake, Riley's smile
stretched from whisker to whisker.
Willow Valley really was the *best* place
to live in the whole wide world. . .

Look out for more

stories – out now!

WILLOW VALLEY

Birthday Fun
Tracey Corderoy

"I wish I lived in Willow Valley"
Philippa Forrester

WILLOW VALLEY

Spooky Sleepover
Tracey Corderoy

"I wish I lived in Willow Valley"
Philippa Forrester

WILLOW VALLEY

The Big Bike Race
Tracey Corderoy

"I wish I lived in Willow Valley"
Philippa Forrester

WILLOW VALLEY

Hide and Seek
Tracey Corderoy

"I wish I lived in Willow Valley"
Philippa Forrester

WILLOW VALLEY

One Snowy Day
Tracey Corderoy

"I wish I lived in Willow Valley"
Philippa Forrester

WILLOW VALLEY

A Seaside Rescue
Tracey Corderoy

"I wish I lived in Willow Valley"
Philippa Forrester

WILLOW VALLEY

Toffee Apple Night
Tracey Corderoy

"I wish I lived in Willow Valley"
Philippa Forrester